I0534023

Turning Point

Turning Point
ALFRED COPPEL

ÆGYPAN PRESS

From *If: Worlds of Science Fiction* November 1953.

Special thanks to Sankar Viswanathan, Greg Weeks, and the
Online Distributed Proofreading Team (which can be found
at http://www.pgdp.net).

Turning Point
A publication of
ÆGYPAN PRESS

www.aegypan.com

The man is rare who will give his life for what is merely the lesser of two evils. Merrick's decision was even tougher: to save human beings at the expense of humanity, or vice versa?

This, then, was the Creche, Anno Domini 2500. A great, mile-square blind cube topping a ragged mountain; bare escarpments falling away to a turbulent sea. For five centuries the Creche had stood so, and the Androids had come forth in an unending stream to labor for Man, the Master. . . .
— Quintus Bland, The Romance of Genus Homo

*D*irector Han Merrick paced the floor nervously. His thin, almost ascetic face was pale and drawn.

"We can't allow it, Virginia," he said, "Prying of this sort can only precipitate a pogrom or worse. Erikson is a bigot of the worst kind. The danger —" He broke off helplessly.

His wife shook her head slowly. "It cannot be prevented, Han. Someone was bound to start asking questions sooner or later. History should have taught us that. And five hundred years of secrecy was more than anyone had a right to expect. Nothing lasts forever."

The trouble is, Merrick told himself, *simply that I am the wrong man for this job. I should never have taken it. There's a wrongness in what we are doing here that colors my every reaction and makes me incapable of acting on my own.*

*Always the doubts and secret questioning. If the social struc-
ture of our world weren't moribund, I wouldn't be here at
all. . . .*

"History, Virginia," he said, "can't explain what
there is no precedent for. The Creche is unique in
human experience."

"The Creche may be, Han, but Sweyn Erikson is not.
Consider his background and tell me if there hasn't
been an Erikson in every era of recorded history. He
is merely another obstacle in the path of progress that
must be overcome. The job is yours, Han."

"A pleasant prospect," Merrick replied bleakly. "I am
an organizer, not a psychotechnician. How am I sup-
posed to protect the Creche from the likes of Erikson?
What insanity bore this fruit, Virginia? The Prophet,
the number one Fanatic, coming here as an *investigator*
in the name of the Council of Ten! I realize the Council
turns pale at the thought of the vote the Fanatics
control, but surely *something* could have been done!
Have those idiots forgotten what we do here? Is that
possible?"

Virginia Merrick shook her head. "The stone got too
hot for them to handle, so they've thrown it to you."

"But Erikson, himself! The very man who organized
the Human Supremacy Party and the Antirobot
League! If he sets foot within the Creche it will mean
an end to everything!"

The woman lit a cigarette and inhaled deeply. "We
can't keep him out and you know it. There's an army
of Fanatics gathering out there in the hills this very
minute. Armed with cortical-stimulant projectors,
Han. That isn't a pleasant way to die —"

Merrick studied his wife carefully. There was fear
under her iron control. She was thinking of the shattering pain of death under the projectors. Nothing else,
really. The Creche didn't matter to her. The Creche

didn't really matter to any of the staff. Three hundred years ago it would have been different. The custodians of the Creche would have gladly died to preserve their trust in those times. . . .

What irony, Merrick thought, that it should come like this. He knew what the projectors did to men. He also knew what they did to robots.

"If they dare to use their weapons on us it will wipe out every vestige of control work done here since the beginning," he said softly.

"They have no way of knowing that."

"Nor would they believe it if we told them."

"And that brings us right back to where we started. You can't keep Erikson out, and the Council of Ten has left us on our own. They don't dare oppose the Fanatics. But there's an old political maxim you would do well to consider very carefully since it's our only hope, Han," Virginia Merrick said, "'If you can't beat someone — join him.'"

*S*he dragged deeply on her cigarette, blue smoke curling from her gold-tinted lips. "This has been coming on for ten years. I tried to warn you then, but you wouldn't listen. Remember?"

How like a woman, Merrick thought bitterly, to be saying I told you so.

"What would you have me do, Virginia?" he asked, "Help the bigot peddle his robot-hate? That can't be the way. Don't you feel anything at all when the reports of pogroms come in?"

Virginia Merrick shrugged. "Better they than we, Han."

"Has it occurred to you that our whole culture might collapse if Erikson has his way?"

"Antirobotism is natural to human beings. Compromise is the only answer. Precautions have to be taken —"

"Precautions!" exploded Merrick. "What sort of precautions can be taken against pure idiocy?"

"The founding board of Psychotechnicians —"

"No help from that source. You know that I've always felt the whole premise was questionable. On the grounds of common fairness, if nothing else."

"Really, Han," Virginia snapped, "It was the only thing to do and you know it. The Creche is the only safeguard the race has."

"Now you sound like the Prophet. In reverse."

"We needn't argue the point."

"No, I suppose not," the Director muttered.

"Then what are you going to do when he gets here?" She ground out her cigarette anxiously. "The procession is in the ravine now. You had better decide quickly."

"I don't know, Virginia. I just don't know." Merrick sank down behind his desk, hands toying with the telescreen controls. "I was never intended to make this sort of decisions. I feel helpless. Look here —"

The image of the ravine glowed across the screen in brilliant relief. The densely timbered slopes were spotted with tiny purposeful figures in the grey robes that all Fanatics affected. Here and there the morning sun caught a glint of metal as the Fanatics labored to set up their projectors. Along the floor of the ravine that was the only land approach to the Creche moved the twisting, writhing snake of the procession. The enraptured Fanatics were chanting their hate-songs as they came. In the first rank walked the leonine Erikson, his long hair whipping in the moisture-laden wind from the sea.

With a muttered curse, Merrick flipped a toggle and the scene dimmed. The face of a secretary appeared superimposed on it. It was the expressionless face of an android, a fine example of the Creche's production line. "Get Graves up here," he ordered, "You may find him at Hypno-Central or in Semantic Evaluation."

"Very good, sir," intoned the android, fading from the screen.

Merrick looked at his wife. "Maybe Graves and I can think of something."

"Don't plan anything rash, Han."

Merrick shrugged and turned back to watch the steady approach of the procession of grey-frocked zealots in the ravine.

Graves appeared as the doorway dilated. He looked fearful and pale. "You wanted to see me, Han?"

"Come in, Jon. Sit down."

"Have you seen the projectors those crackpots have set up in the hills?" Graves demanded.

"I have, Jon. That's what I wanted to talk to you about."

"My God, Han! Do you have any idea of what it must feel like to die from cortical stimulation?" Graves' voice was tense and strained. "Can't we get out of here by 'copter?"

"No. The 'copters are both in Francisco picking up supplies. I ordered them out yesterday. Besides, that wouldn't settle anything. There are almost a thousand androids in the Creche as of this morning. What about them?"

Graves made a gesture of impatience. "It's the humans I'm thinking about."

Merrick forced down the bitter taste of disgust that welled into his throat and forced himself to go on. "We have to take some sort of action to protect the Creche, Jon. I've held off until the last moment, thinking the

Council would never allow a Fanatic to investigate the Creche, but the Ten are more afraid of the HSP rubber stamp vote than they are of letting a thousand androids be slaughtered. But we can't leave it at that. If we don't prevent it, Erikson will precipitate a pogrom that will make the Canalopolis massacre look like a tea-party." For some reason he held back the information about the effect of the Fanatic weapon on robot tissue. The vague notion that knowing, Jon Graves might cast his lot with Erikson, restrained him.

"Of course, Erikson will come in wearing an energy shield," Graves said.

"He will. And we have none," Virginia Merrick said softly.

"Can we compromise with him?" Graves asked.

There it was again, Merrick thought, the weasel-word 'compromise.' There was a moral decay setting in everywhere — the founders of the Creche would never have spoken so. "No," he said flatly, "We cannot. Erikson has conceived a robot-menace. All the old hate-patterns are being dusted off and used on the rabble. People are actually asking one another if they would like their daughters to *marry* robots. That sort of thing, as old as *homo sapiens*. And one cannot compromise with prejudice. It seduces the emotions and dulls the mind. No, there will be no appeasing of Sweyn Erikson or his grey-shirted nightriders!"

"You're talking like a starry-eyed fool, Han," Virginia Merrick said sharply.

"Can't we take him in and give him the works?" Graves asked hopefully. "Primary Conditioning could handle the job. Give him a fill-in with false memory?"

Merrick shook his head. "We can't risk narcosynthesis and that's essential. He'll surely be tested for blood purity when he leaves, and scopolamine traces would be a dead give-away that we had been trying to hide something here."

"Then it looks as though compromise is the only way, Han. They've got us up against the wall. See here, Han, I know you don't agree, but what else is there? After all, we all believe in human supremacy. Erikson calls it a robot-menace, we look at it from another angle, but our common goal is the betterment of the human culture we've established. People are on an emotional jag now. There has been no war for five centuries. No emotional release. And there have been regulations and conventions set up since the Atom War that only a very few officials have been allowed to understand. Erikson is no savage, Han, after all. True he's set off a rash of robot-baiting, but he can be dealt with on an intelligent plane, I'm sure."

"He is a man of ability, you know," Virginia Merrick said.

"Ability," Merrick said bitterly. "Rabble rouser and bigot! Look at his record. Organizer of the riots in Low Chicago. Leader in the Antirobot Labor League — the same outfit that slaughtered fifty robots in the Tycho dock strike. Think, you two! To tell such a man what the Creche is would be to tie a rope around the neck of every android alive. Lynch law! The rope and the whip for every one of them. And then suppose the worm turns? *It can, you know!* Our methods here are far from perfect. What then?"

"I still say we must compromise," Graves said. "They will kill us if we don't —"

"He's no troglodyte, Han, I'm certain —" Merrick's wife said plaintively.

The Director felt resistance flowing out of him. They were right, of course. There was nothing else he could do.

"All right," Merrick's voice was low and tired. He felt the weight of his years settling down on him. "I'll do as you suggest. I'll try to lead him off the trail first —" that was his compromise with himself, he knew, and he hated himself for it — "and if I fail I'll tell him the whole truth."

He flipped the telescreen toggle in time to see Sweyn Erikson detach himself from his followers and disappear through the dilated outer gate in the side of the Creche. A faint, almost futile stirring of defiance shook him. He found himself in the anomalous position of wanting to defend something that he had long felt was wrong in concept from the beginning — and not being able to take an effective course of action.

He reached into his desk drawer and took out an ancient automatic. It was a family heirloom, heavy, black and deadly. He pulled back the slide and watched one of the still-bright brass cartridges snap up into the breech. He handled the weapon awkwardly, but as he slipped it into his jumper pocket some of the weariness slipped from him and a cold anger took its place. He looked calmly from his wife to Graves.

"I'll tell him the whole truth," he said, "And if he fails to react as you two think he will, I shall kill him."

Sweyn Erikson, in a pre-Atom War culture, might have been a dictator. But the devastation of the war had at long last resulted in a peaceful world-state, and where no nations exist, politics becomes a sterile business of direction and supervision. It is war or the threat of war that gives a politician his power. Sweyn Erikson wanted power above all else. And so he founded a religion.

He became the Prophet of the Fanatics. And since a cult must have an object of group hate as a *raison-d'etre*, he chose the androids. With efficiency and calculated sincerity, he beat the drums of prejudice until his organization had spread its influence into the world's high places and his word became the law of the land.

People who beheld his feral magnificence, and listened to the spell-binding magic of his oratory — followed. His power sprang from the masses — unthinking, emotional. He gave the mob a voice and a purpose. He was like a Hitler or a Torquemada. Like a Long or a John Brown. He was savage and rapacious, courageous and bitter. He was Man.

There were four cardinal precepts by which the membership of the Human Supremacy Party lived. First, Man was God. Second, no race could share the plenum with Man. Had separate races still remained after the Atom War, the HSP racism might have been more specific, but since there remained only humanity en masse, all human beings shared the godhead. Third, the artificial persons that streamed from the Creche were blasphemy. Fourth, they must be destroyed. Like other generations before them, the humans of this age rallied to the banner of the whip and the rope. Not since the War had blood been spilled, but the destructive madness of homo sapiens found joy in the word of the Prophet, and though the blood was only the red sap of androids, the thrill was there.

Thus had Sweyn Erikson, riding the intolerant wave of antirobotism, come to the Creche. He stood now, in the long bare foyer, waiting. Behind him lay the Party and the League. The Council of Ten was in hand and helpless. Upon his report to the world, the future of an entire robot-human culture pattern rested. This, he told himself, was the high point of his life. Naked power to use as he chose rested in his hands. The whole structure of world society was tottering. The choice was his and his alone. He could shore it up or shatter it and trample on the fragments. . . .

The Prophet savored the moment. He watched with interest as the door before him dilated. The Creche Director stood eyeing him half-fearfully, half-defiantly, flanked by his wife and his assistant. They were all three afraid for their lives, Erikson thought with satisfaction.

"We welcome you to the Creche," Han Merrick said formally.

"Let there be no ceremony," Erikson said, "I am a simple man."

Merrick's lips tightened. "You haven't come here for ceremony. There will be none."

"I came for truth," the Prophet said sonorously. "The people of the world are waiting for my words. The mask of secrecy must be ripped from this place and truth and knowledge allowed to wash it clean."

Merrick almost winced. The statement was redundant with the propaganda that Erikson's nightriders peddled on every street corner. It betokened an intellectual bankruptcy among men that was frightening.

"I shall do my best to allay your fears," he said thickly.

Erikson's eyes glittered with suspicion. "I need only a guide. The decisions I shall make for myself. And mind that I am shown every concealed place. The roots of this place must be laid bare. 'For God shall bring every work into judgment, with every secret thing; whether it be good or whether it be evil.' The Scriptures command it in the name of Man, the True God."

Twisted, pious, hypocrite! thought Merrick.

"I am sure, sir," Graves was saying placatingly, "that when we have shown you the Creche you will see that there is no menace."

Erikson scowled at Graves deliberately. "There is menace enough in the blasphemy of android life, my son. Everywhere there are signs of unrest among the things you have built here. On Mars, human beings have died at their hands!"

Merrick's face showed his disgust. "Frankly, I don't believe that. Androids don't kill."

"We shall see, my son," Erikson said settling the belt of his energy screen more comfortably about his hips. "We shall see."

Merrick studied Erikson's face. There was a tiny scar under his chin. That would be where the transmitter was planted. He had no doubt that every word of this conversation was being monitored by the Fanatics outside the Creche. The turning point was coming inexorably nearer. He only hoped that he had the physical and moral courage to face it when it arrived.

"Very well, Sweyn Erikson," he said finally. "Please come with me."

*F*our hours later they were in Merrick's office. The preliminary stage of his plan had failed, just as he had known it would. He was almost glad. It had been a vacillating expediency, an attempt to hide the facts and avoid the necessity of facing the challenge squarely. Stage two was about to begin, and this time there would be no temporizing.

The Prophet glared angrily across the desk-top. "Do you take me for a child? You have shown me nothing. Where are the protoplasm vats? The brain machines? Where are the bodies assembled? I warned you against trickery, Han Merrick!"

Merrick glanced across the room at his wife. She sat rigid in her chair, her face a pale mask. He would get no help from her.

"You must realize, Erikson," he said, "That you are forcing me to jeopardize five centuries of work for the chimera of Human Supremacy. Let me warn you now that your life is of no importance to me when balanced against that. When the Board of Psychotechnicians appointed my family custodians of the Creche centuries ago, they did so because they knew we would keep faith —"

"The last member of the founding Board died more than two hundred years ago," snapped the Prophet.

"But the Creche is here, and I am here to guard it as my forefathers did," Merrick said. Once again he was conscious of a strange ambivalence in his attitude. He must guard something he considered wrong against the intrusion of a danger even more wrong. His hand sought the scored grip of the old automatic in his pocket. Could he actually kill?

"You speak of Human Supremacy as a chimera," Sweyn Erikson said, "It is no such thing. It is the only vital force left in the world. Robotism is a menace more deadly, a blasphemy more foul than any Black Mass of history. You are making Man into an anachronism on the face of his own planet. This cannot be! *I* will not let it be. . . ."

Merrick stared. Could it be that the man actually believed that the poison he peddled was the food of the gods?

"I will try one last attempt at reason, Erikson," Merrick said deliberately. "Look back with an unprejudiced mind, if you can, over the centuries since the Atom War. What do you see?"

"I see Man emasculated by the robot!"

"No! You see atomic power harnessed and in use for the first time after almost a millenium of muddling. You see Man standing on the Moon and the habitable planets — and soon to reach out for the stars! A new Golden Age is dawning, Prophet! And why? Whence have come the techniques?" Even as he spoke, Merrick knew he was ignoring the obvious, the all-too-apparent cracks in the social structure that no scientific miracles could cure. But were those cracks the fault of robotism or were they in fact a failing inherent in Man himself? He was not prepared to answer that. "From where are the techniques drawn?" he asked again.

Erikson met his glance squarely. "Not from the mindless horrors you spawn here!"

"Emotionless, Prophet," corrected Merrick pointedly, "Not mindless."

"Soulless! Soulless and mindless, too. Never have these zombies been able to think as men!"

"They are not men."

"Nor are they the architects of the future!"

"I think you are wrong, Prophet," Merrick said softly.

"Man is the ultimate," Erikson said.

"You talk like a fool," snapped Merrick.

"*Han!*" There was naked terror in his wife's voice, but he rushed on, ignoring it.

"How dare you say that Man is the ultimate? What right have you to assume that nature has stopped experimenting?"

Sweyn Erikson's lip curled scornfully. "Can you be implying that the robots —"

Merrick leaned across the desk to shout full in the Prophet's face: *"You fool! They're not robots!"*

The robed man was suddenly on his feet, face livid.

"Han!" cried Virginia Merrick, "Not that way!"

"This is my affair now, Virginia. I'll handle it in my own way!" the Director said.

"Remember the mob outside!"

Merrick turned agate-hard eyes on his wife. Presently he looked away and said to the Prophet. "Now I will show you the real Creche!"

*T*here were robots everywhere — blank-eyed, like sleep walkers. They reacted to commands. They moved and breathed and fed themselves. Under rigid control they performed miracles of intuitive calculation. But artificiality was stamped upon them like a brand. They were *not* human.

In the lowest vaults of the Creche, Merrick showed the Prophet the infants. He withheld nothing. He showed him the growing creatures. He explained to him the tests and signs that were looked for in the hospitals maintained by the World State and the Council of Ten. He let him watch the young ones taking their Primary Conditioning. Courses of hypnotic instruction. Rest, narcosynthesis. Semantics. Drugs and words and more words pounding on young brains like sledgehammer blows, shaping them into something acceptable in a sapient world.

In other chambers, other age groups. Emotion and memory being molded into something else by hypnopedia. Faces becoming blank and expressionless.

"Their minds are conditioned — enslaved," Merrick said bitterly. "Then they are primed with scientific facts. Those techniques we discussed. *This* is where they come from, Prophet. From the minds of your despised androids. Only will is suppressed, and emotion. They are shaped for the sociography of a sapient culture. They mature very slowly. We keep them here for from

ten to fifteen years. No human brain could stand it —
but *theirs* can."

Truth dangled before his eyes, but Erikson's mind
savagely rejected it. The pillars upon which he had built
his life were crumbling. . . .

The two men stood in a vast hall filled with an
insidious, whispering voice. On low pallets, fully a
score of physically mature androids lay staring vacu-
ously at a spinning crystal high in the apex of the
domed ceiling.

"— you had no life before you where created here to
serve Man the master you had no life before you were
created here to serve Man the master you had —" the
voice whispered into the hypnotized brains.

"Don't look up," Merrick warned. "The crystal can
catch a human being faster than it can *them*. This is
hypnotic engineering. The rhythm of the syllables and
their proportion to the length of word and sentence
are computed to correspond to typed encepha-
lographic curves. Nothing is left to chance. When they
have reached this stage of conditioning they are almost
ready for release and purchase by human beings. Only
a severe stimulation of the brain can break down the
walls we have built in their minds."

Erikson made a gesture as though darkness were
streaking his vision. He was shaken badly. "But where
do they — where do they come from?"

"The State maternity hospitals, of course," Merrick
said, "Where else? The parents are then sterilized by
the Health and Welfare Authority as an added safeguard. Births occur at a ratio of about one for every
six million normals." He smiled mirthlessly at the
Prophet of Human Supremacy. "Well? Little man, what
now?"

Honest realization still refused to come. It needed
to be put into words, and Sweyn Erikson had no such

words. "I see only that you are taking children of men and disfiguring —"

"For the last time," gritted Merrick, "These are *not* human beings. Genus homo, yes. *Homo chaos,* if you choose. But not homo sapiens. I think of them," he said with sudden calm, "As *Homo Supremus.* The next step on the evolutionary ladder. . . ."

At last the words had been spoken and the flood gates were down in the tortured brain of the Prophet. Like a sudden conflagration, realization came — and with it, blind terror.

"No! Nonono! You cannot continue this devil's work! Think what it would mean if these things should ever be loosed on the world of Man!" the Prophet's voice was a steadily rising shrill of fear.

Han Merrick looked out across the rows of pallets, each with its burden of a superman, bound like Prometheus to the rock, helpless in hypnotic chains. It struck him again that his life had not been well spent. He looked from his charges to the ranting fear-crazed rabble-rouser. The contrast was too shocking, too complete. For the "androids" were, in fact, worthy of a dignity even in slavery that homo sapiens had never attained in overlordship. Merrick knew at last what he must do.

Racial loyalty stirred, but was quickly smothered in the humiliation of man's omnipresent thievery. For it *was* thievery, Merrick thought. Man was keeping for himself the heritage that was the rightful property of a newer, better race.

He took the automatic from his jumper and leveled it at Erikson's chest. He felt very sure and right. Though he knew that he was sealing the death warrant of his wife and his friends, the memory of their vacillations anesthetized him against any feeling of loss. He waited until Erikson screamed one word into the transmitter imbedded in his flesh —

The word was: *"Attack!"*

— and in the next instant, Han Merrick shot him dead.

*T*he fanatics on the ridges heard the Prophet's command and sprang to comply. Energy swept out of the grids, through the coils of the projectors and out over the blind cube of the Creche.

Han Merrick felt the first radiations. He felt the beginnings of cortical hypertrophy and screamed. Every synapse sagged under the increasing load of sensitivity. The pressure of the air became an unbearable burden, the faintest sound became a shattering roar. Every microscopic pain, every cellular process became a rending, tearing agony. He screamed and the sound was a cataclysmic, planet-smashing hell of noise within his skull. He sagged to the floor and thinking stopped. He contracted himself, pulling legs and arms inward in a massive convulsion until at last he had assumed the foetal position. After a long while, he died.

Every human being within the Creche died so, but there was still life. The energy that killed the lesser creature freed the greater — just as Merrick had known it would. Unhuman matter pulsed under the caressing rain. A thousand beings shuddered at the sudden release of their chains. The speakers ranted unheard. The crystals turned unwatched. The bonds forged by homo sapiens snapped and there came —

Maturity.

This, now, is the Creche, Anno Domini 3000. A great mile-square blind cube topping a ragged mountain; bare escarpments falling away to a turbulent sea. For ten centuries the Creche has stood so, and the Androids still come forth, now to lift their starships to the Magellanic Clouds and beyond. A Golden Age has come. But, of course, Man is no longer the Master.
    — *Quintus Bland, The Romance of Genus Homo.*
THE END

www.ingramcontent.com/pod-product-compliance
Lightning Source LLC
Chambersburg PA
CBHW031906170626
46807CB00004B/1922